W9-BPL-044

A Note to Parents and Teachers

The *Dorling Kindersley Readers* series is a reading program for children which is highly respected by teachers and educators around the world. The LEGO Company has a global reputation for offering high-quality, innovative products, specially designed to stimulate a child's creativity and development through play.

Now Dorling Kindersley has joined forces with The LEGO Company to produce the first-ever graded reading program to be based around LEGO play themes. Each *Dorling Kindersley Reader* is guaranteed to capture a child's imagination, while developing his or her reading skills, general knowledge, and love of reading.

The books are written and designed in conjunction with literacy experts, including Dr. Linda Gambrell, President of the National Reading Conference and past board member of the International Reading Association.

The four levels of *Dorling Kindersley Readers* are aimed at different reading abilities, enabling you to choose the books that are right for each child.

Level 1 – Beginning to Read
Level 2 – Beginning to Read Alone
Level 3 – Reading Alone
Level 4 – Proficient Readers

The "normal" age at which a child begins to read can be from three to eight years old, so these levels are only guidelines.

Dorling Kindersley

LONDON, NEW YORK, SYDNEY, DELHI, PARIS,
MUNICH and JOHANNESBURG

Senior Editor Cynthia O'Neill
Senior Art Editor Nick Avery
Senior Managing Editor Karen Dolan
Managing Art Editor Cathy Tincknell
DTP Designer Jill Bunyan
Production Chris Avgherinos
US Editor Gary Werner
Reading Consultant
Linda B. Gambrell, Ph.D

First American Edition, 2000
2 4 6 8 10 9 7 5 3 1
Published in the United States by Dorling Kindersley Publishing, Inc.
95 Madison Avenue, New York, New York 10016

www.lego.com

Library of Congress Cataloging-in-Publication Data
Baxter, Nicola
Castle under attack / by Nicola Baxter. -- 1st American ed.
p. cm. -- (Dorling Kindersley readers)
Summary: As King Leo is hosting a feast at the LEGO castle, the outlaw
Cedric launches an attack and takes Princess Storm hostage.
ISBN 0-7894-5460-2 (pbk.) -- ISBN 0-7894-6094-7 (hc.)
[1. Castles--Fiction. 2. Adventure and adventurers--Fiction.] I. Title.
II. Series.

PZ7.B3377 Cas 2000
[Fic]--dc21
99-055202

Color reproduction by Dot Gradations, UK
Printed and bound by L Rex, China

The publisher would like to thank the following for their kind
permission to reproduce their photographs:
c=center; b=bottom; l=left; r=right; t=top

E.T. Archive: 25br;
Mary Evans Picture Library: 11tr, 12br;
Robert Harding Picture Library: Roy Rainford 7br, 32crb.

For our complete
catalog visit
www.dk.com

DORLING KINDERSLEY *READERS*

CASTLE
UNDER
ATTACK

Written by Nicola Baxter • Illustrated by Roger Harris

BEGINNING **2** TO READ ALONE

A Dorling Kindersley Book

In a faraway land,
in the middle of a dark forest,
there was a mighty castle.

King Leo and Queen Leonora
lived in the castle
with their daughter, Princess Storm.

One day, the king decided
to hold a feast at the castle.
There would be a tournament
where knights could show their skill.

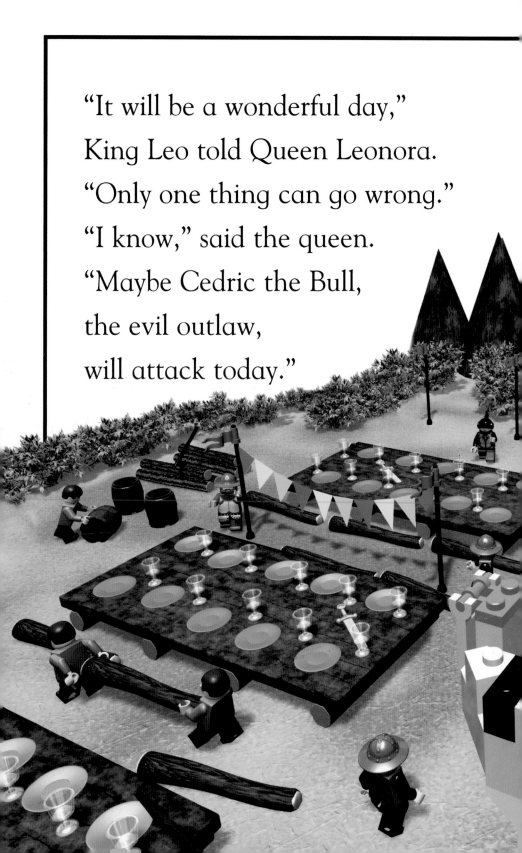

"It will be a wonderful day,"
King Leo told Queen Leonora.
"Only one thing can go wrong."
"I know," said the queen.
"Maybe Cedric the Bull,
the evil outlaw,
will attack today."

King Leo nodded.
"We must be ready,"
he said.

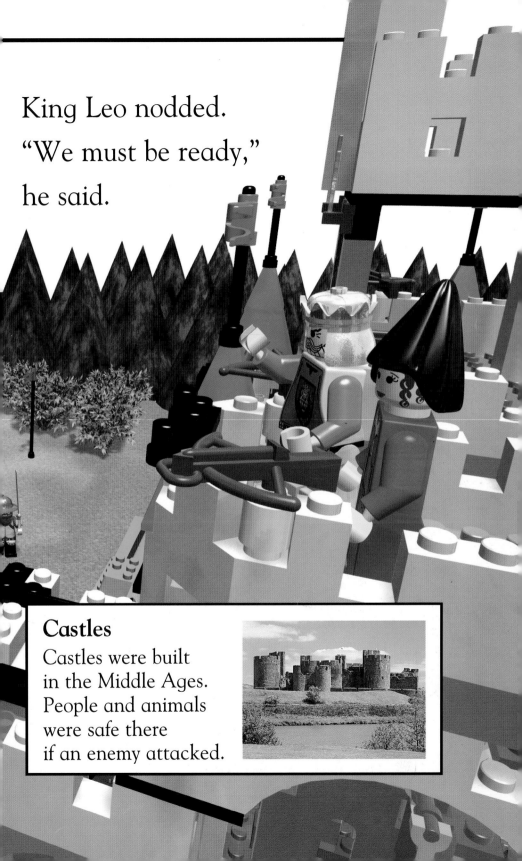

Castles

Castles were built
in the Middle Ages.
People and animals
were safe there
if an enemy attacked.

It was almost time for the feast.

Knights put on their armor.

Children washed at the well.

Armor

Knights wore armor made of iron and steel for protection. Special hinges let them move their arms and legs!

Cedric the Bull watched
from the dark forest.
He could see everyone
getting ready.
"Not long now," he told his deputy,
Gilbert the Bad.

"Let the tournament begin!"
called King Leo.
Richard the Strong took part
in the first contest.
The horses galloped forward.
The weapons clashed.
Sir Richard won.
"Well done!"
cheered the king.

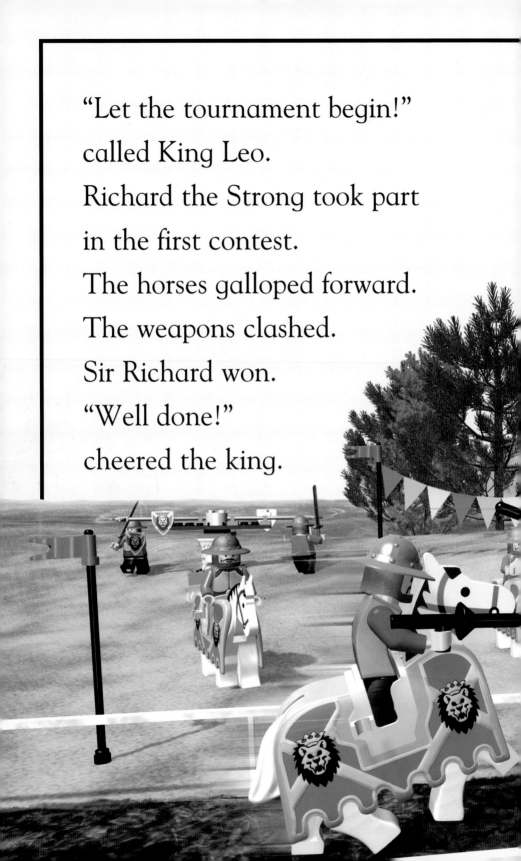

Tournaments

In peacetime, knights trained by taking part in pretend battles, called tournaments. Some fought with long spears, called lances.

Cedric the Bull and Gilbert the Bad
hid behind the castle.

They had pushed an attack tower
up to the thick wall.

"Why did you make it so heavy?"
puffed Cedric.

"It has to carry twenty men,"
said Gilbert.

"We need it to climb the castle wall.
Then we can capture the castle!"

Attack!

Careful planning was
needed for a surprise
attack. Armies could
not move quickly
as the soldiers wore
heavy armor and used
huge weapons.

King Leo was cheering the knights
when he heard a bugle call
above the noise of the crowd.

"It's the signal," he told his family.

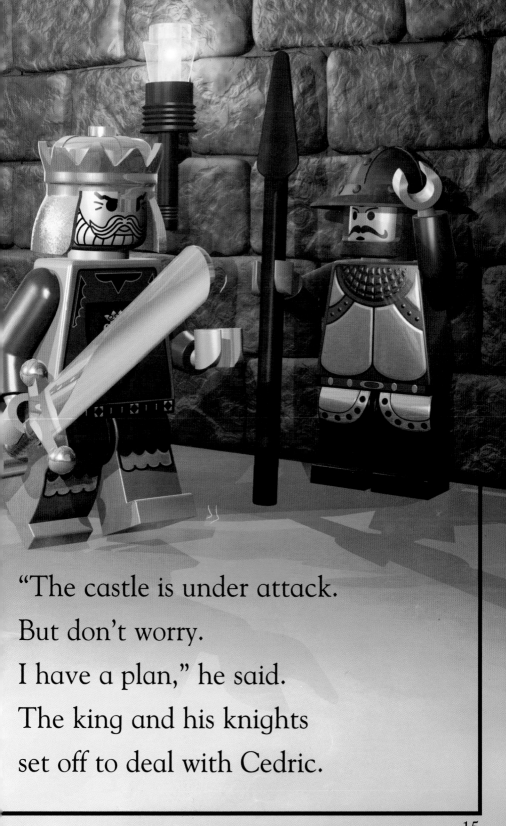

"The castle is under attack.
But don't worry.
I have a plan," he said.
The king and his knights
set off to deal with Cedric.

Cedric was a cowardly leader.
He did not really want to lead
his men up the tower.
"You must come, too,"
he told Gilbert.

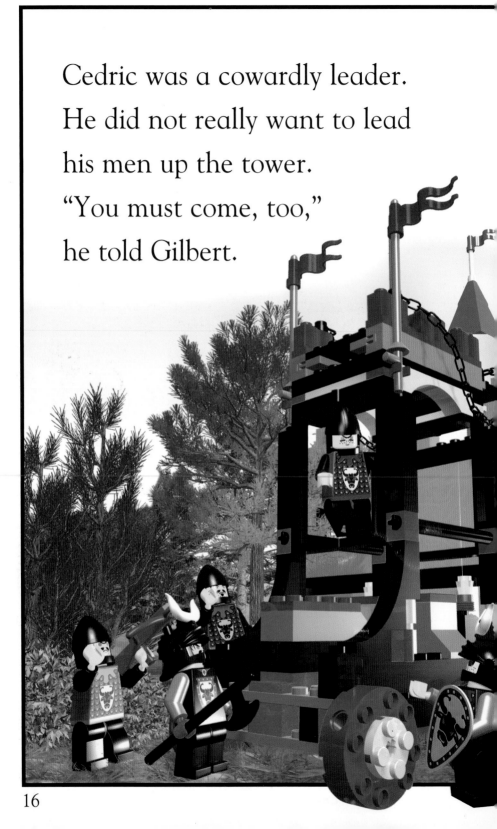

The outlaws climbed the tower.
"Nearly there," panted Cedric.
He looked up.
"Oh no! Yuk!"
he cried.
Smelly food and
horse droppings
poured onto the
outlaws' heads.

On top of the castle,
King Leo smiled.
"What a good plan,"
he laughed.

The king and his knights
went to the Great Hall.
The queen was waiting for them,
but Princess Storm was missing.
"Where's my daughter?"
the king asked.

A knight slipped away.
He was called
John of Mayne,
and the princess
was his friend.
He thought
he knew where
to find her.

Near the forest,
there was a garden.
It was where
the princess sat
when she felt sad.

Storm was unhappy because
she wanted to be a knight
and help her father King Leo.
But girls were not allowed
to be knights.

Women
Women did not have
much power. But when
the men were away
fighting, the women did
their work!

John could see the princess
sitting in the garden.
Before he could call to her,
someone appeared from the trees.
It was Gilbert the Bad.
He pulled Storm into the forest.

Gilbert took the princess
to the outlaws' hidden camp,
where Cedric was waiting.

"I'm not afraid of you,"
said Storm, bravely.
"I don't care," replied Cedric.
"I want the king's money.
Your father will pay me a high price
for your safe return."

Forests

In the Middle Ages,
forests were much
bigger than they are
now. Wood from the
trees was used to build
carts, ships, and homes.

A bugle call rang out in the forest.
It was a signal to Cedric.
"The king himself is looking
for you!" he told Storm.

"While the king searches the forest, my outlaws will attack his castle!" said Cedric.

He sat down with Gilbert to plan the attack.

An outlaw kept watch in the treetops.

"I can see the king!" he called. "He is lost in the forest. It will take him hours to find his way out!"

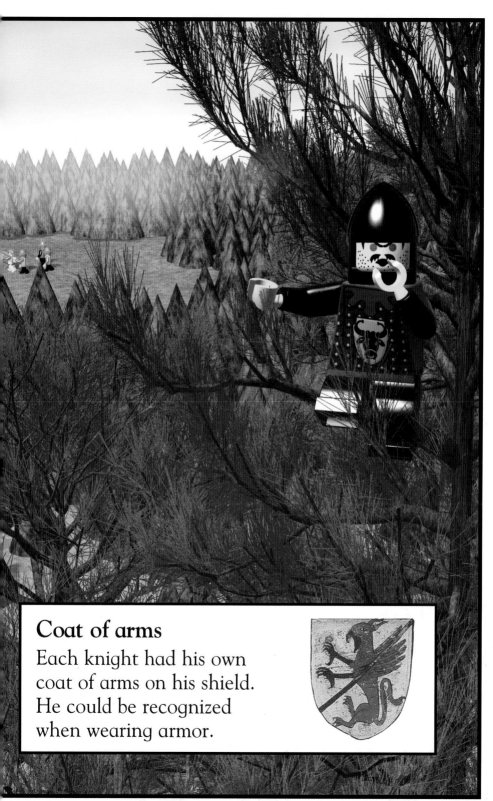

Coat of arms
Each knight had his own coat of arms on his shield. He could be recognized when wearing armor.

Cedric and Gilbert were plotting,
and they forgot to watch the princess.
Storm quietly escaped into the trees.

"She doesn't matter," said Cedric.
"Why ask for a little bit of treasure?
Now we can take it all!"

Soon, Cedric and the outlaws
surrounded the castle.
They loaded a catapult
with a rock.
"Fire!"
said Cedric.

Weapons of war

Swords and lances were no use for attacking a castle. Instead, huge catapults hurled enormous rocks and did serious damage.

Then there came a shout.
The king rode out from the forest.
"You are surrounded!" he cried.
"Give up your weapons."
"We thought you were lost!"
said Cedric.

"It was a clever trick.
Sir Richard is wearing my armor!"
laughed the king.
"Now you are trapped!"

"I still have your daughter!"
Cedric lied to the king.
"Oh no you don't!" called Storm,
running out from the trees.
"Hooray!" cheered the knights.
The outlaws were taken away.

That night, in the dungeons,
the outlaws could hear the feast.
Everyone was very happy,
apart from the outlaws, of course.

"I'm not finished yet,"
Cedric said, in a horrible whisper.
"Just you wait, King Leo!
Just you wait!"

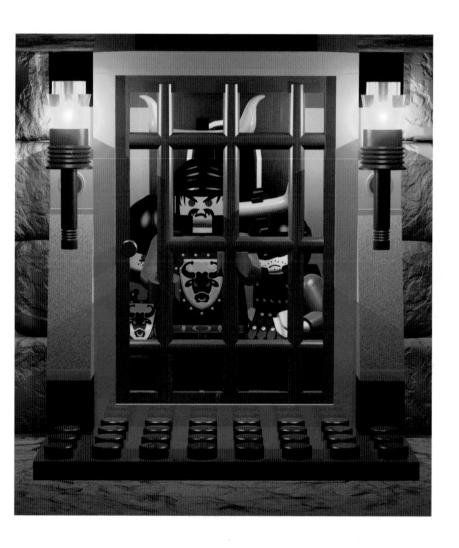

Knights and castles facts

Only boys from rich families were allowed to train as knights.

A boy started training to be a knight at the age of seven.

A knight was a soldier who rode a horse in battle. He fought for a lord or king.

It could take a knight up to one hour to put on all his armor.

Feasts were held in the Great Hall. They started early. People began eating by 11 o'clock in the morning. The meal lasted for hours.

Most castles were built in a time called the Middle Ages. This lasted from around AD 450 to 1500.

A suit of armor cost about $80,000, in today's money. That is more than most sports cars!

The first castles were built of wood. It was easy to burn them down. So then builders started to use stone.